P9-DGI-603

For Antoinette, who knows her p's and q's.

COPYRIGHT © 1998 by Callaway & Kirk Company LLC.
All rights reserved. Published by Scholastic Press, a division of Scholastic Inc., *Publishers since 1920*, in association with Callaway & Kirk Company LLC.
Miss Spider and all related characters are trademarks and/or registered trademarks of Callaway & Kirk Company LLC.
SCHOLASTIC and SCHOLASTIC PRESS and associated logos are trademarks and/or registered trademarks of Scholastic Inc.

Nicholas Callaway, Editorial Director
Antoinette White, Senior Editor · Toshiya Masuda, Designer · True Sims, Production Director
Paula Litzky, Director of Sales & Marketing · Monica Moran, Director of Publicity
Ivan Wong, Jr. and José Rodríguez, Design & Production Associates
Christopher Steighner, Assistant Editor
With thanks to Raphael Shea and Felicity Kate Miller
With special thanks to Heather Dietz at Scholastic Press

No part of this publication may be reproduced in whole or in part, or stored in a retrieval system, or transmitted in any form or by any means, electronic, mechanical, photocopying, recording, or otherwise, without written permission of the publisher.
For information regarding permission, write to Scholastic Inc., Attention: Permissions Department, 555 Broadway, New York, NY 10012.

Library of Congress Cataloging-in-Publication Data
Kirk, David, 1955-
Miss Spider's ABC / paintings and verse by David Kirk
p. cm.
Summary: Jumping june bugs, very vivid violets, entertaining earthworms, and other friends of Miss Spider gather to celebrate her birthday.

ISBN 0-590-28279-4 (alk. paper)
[1. Birthdays—Fiction. 2. Spiders—Fiction. 3. Insects—Fiction. 4. Alphabet.]
I. Title.

PZ7.K63395i 1998
[E]—dc21 97-48415
CIP AC

1 3 5 7 9 10 8 6 4 2

First edition, October 1998
Printed by Palace Press International in Hong Kong

The paintings in this book are oils on paper.

Miss Spider's ABC

paintings and verse by David Kirk

Scholastic Press
Callaway

New York

A

Ants await.

Bumblebees blow balloons.
B

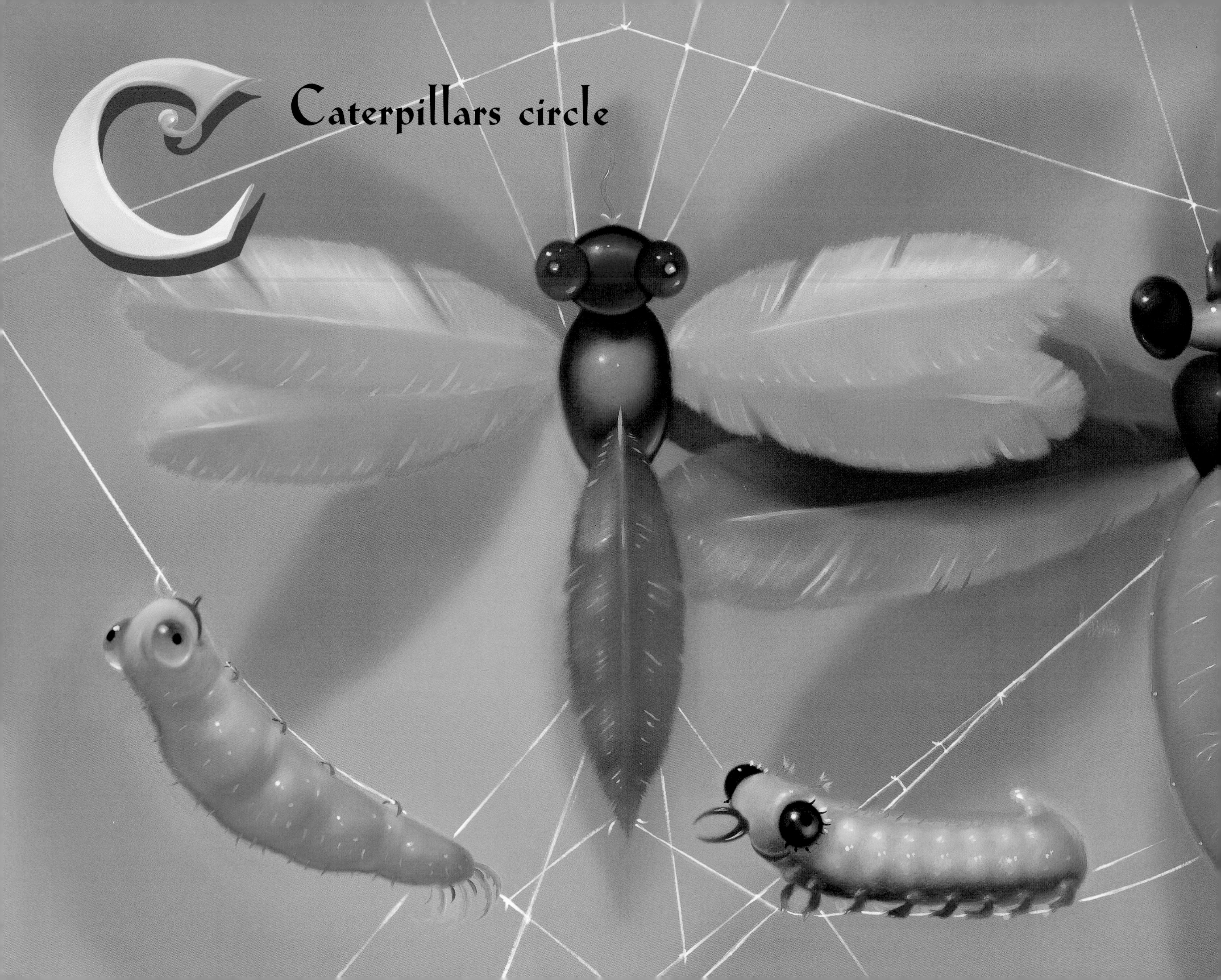

C Caterpillars circle

dragonfly decorations.
D

E

Earthworms entertain.

F

Fireflies fandango.

G

Grasshoppers gaze.

H

Hummingbirds hide

I
inside irises.

J
Jumping june bugs

K
kiss katydids.

L

Ladybugs laugh.

Moths mingle.
M

N

Net-wings nap.

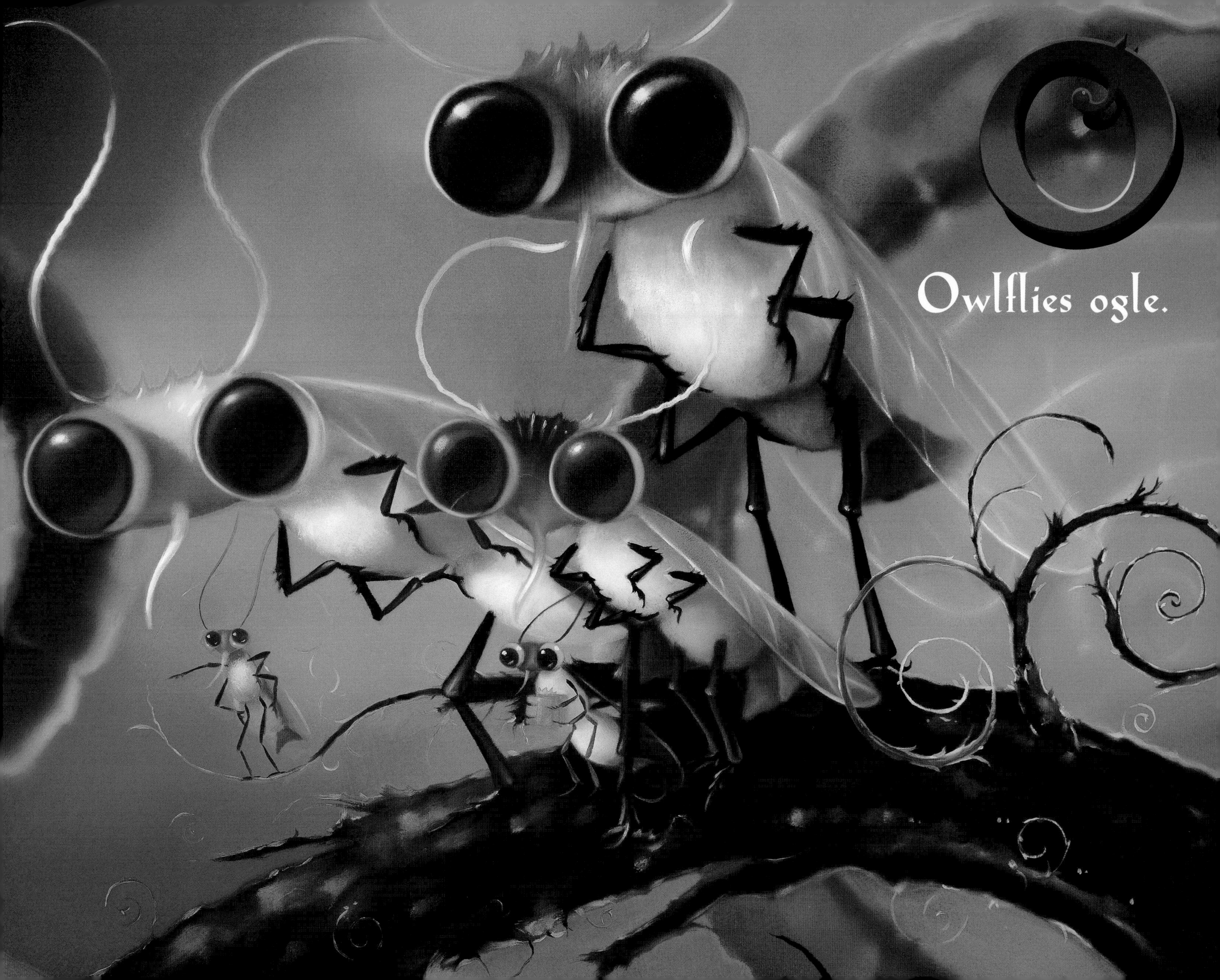

O

Owlflies ogle.

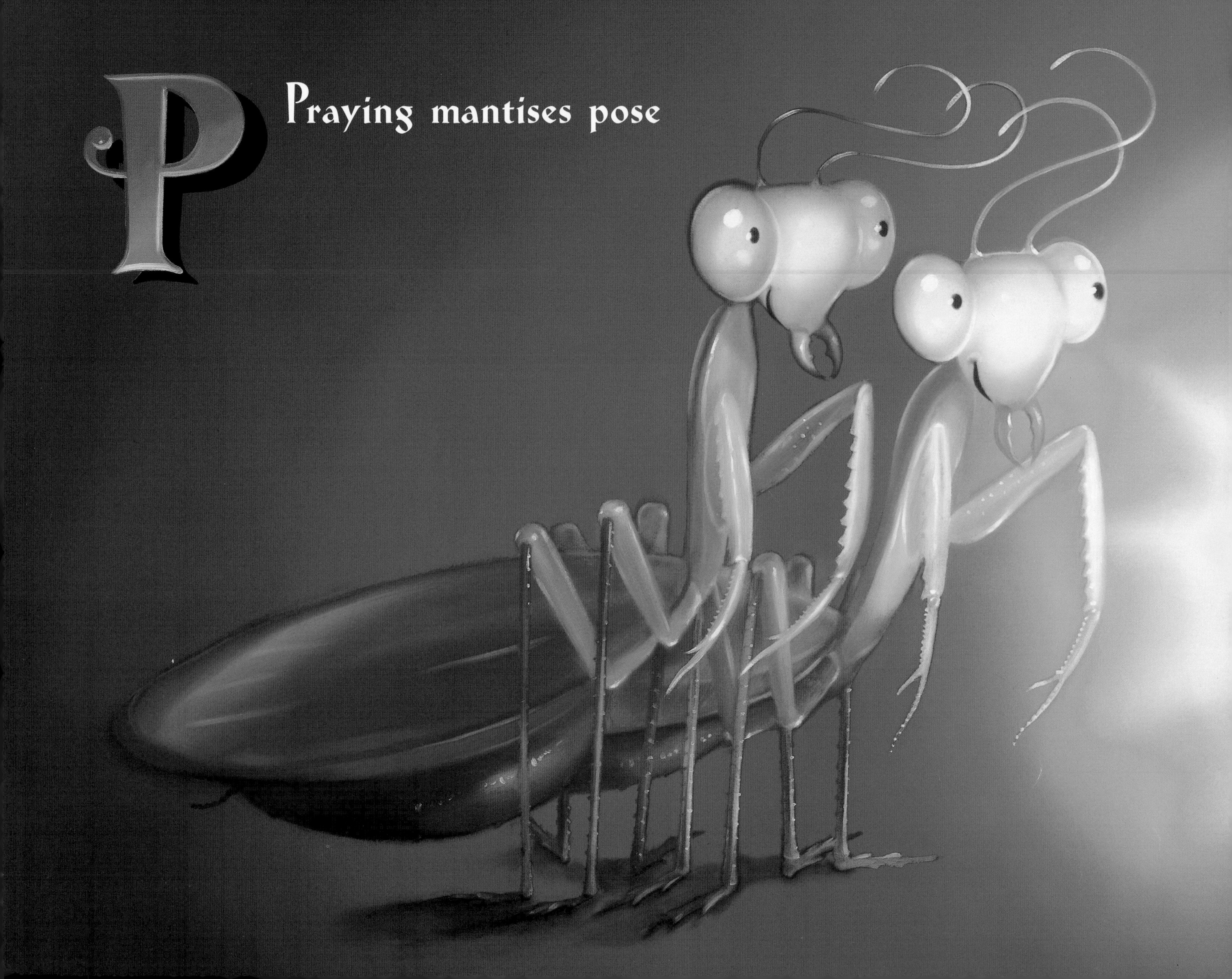

P

Praying mantises pose

for the queen bee.
Q

R

Red roses

S

shelter smiling spiders.

T

Termites tunnel

U

underneath

V
very vivid violets.

W
Walkingsticks

X

make an X.

y
Yellow jackets yield

Z

to the zebra butterfly.

Everyone hides . . .

. . . Shhh . . .

Surprise!
Happy Birthday, Miss Spider!

HAPPY BIRTHDAY MISS SPIDER!

To my
Dearest
Love H.